A NOTE TO PARENTS

One of the most important ways children learn to read—and learn to *like* reading—is by being with readers. Every time you read aloud, read along, or listen to your child read, you are providing the support that she or he needs as an emerging reader.

Disney's First Readers were created to make that reading time fun for you and your child. Each book in this series features characters that most children already recognize from popular Disney films. The familiarity and appeal of these high-interest characters will draw emerging readers easily into the story and at the same time support basic literacy skills, such as understanding that print has meaning, connecting oral language to written language, and developing cueing systems. And because Disney's First Readers are highly visual, children have another tool to help in understanding the text. This makes early reading a comfortable, confident experience—exactly what emerging readers need to become successful, fluent readers.

Read to Your Child

Here are a few hints to make early reading enjoyable and educational:

★ Talk with children before reading. Let them see how much they already know about the Disney characters. If they are unfamiliar with the movie basis of a book, take a few minutes to look at the cover and some of the illustrations to establish a context. Talking is important, since oral language precedes and supports reading.

★ Run your finger along the text to show that the words carry the story. Let your child read along if she or he recognizes that there are repeated words or phrases.

★ Encourage questions. A child's questions are good clues to his or her comprehension or thinking strategies.

★ Be prepared to read the same book several times. Children will develop ease with the story and concepts, so that later they can concentrate on reading and language.

Let Your Child Read to You

You are your child's best audience, so encourage her or him to read aloud to you often. And:

★ If children ask about an unknown word, give it to them. Don't interrupt the flow of reading to have them sound it out. However, if children start to sound out a word, let them.

★ Praise all reading efforts warmly and often!

—Patricia Koppman
Past President
International Reading Association

For Esty, Miriam, and Nechama

Layouts and pencils by Duendes del Sur.

Paintings by Andrea and John Alvin.

Printed in the United States of America.

First Edition

3 5 7 9 10 8 6 4 2

This book is set in 20-point New Aster.

Library of Congress Catalog Card Number: 98-87607

ISBN: 0-7868-4281-4

For more Disney Press fun, visit www.DisneyBooks.com

Tarzan Goes Bananas

by Judy Katschke
Painted by Andrea and John Alvin

A Disney First Reader
A Story from Disney's *Tarzan*

New York

"Have fun today, Tarzan," Kala said.
"And try to stay out of trouble."

Tantor was worried.
"Everything we do leads
to trouble," he said.

Terk had an idea.
"Let's have a banana-picking
contest!"

The friends spread the word
through the jungle.
Terk ran through the trees.
So did Tarzan.

WHOOPS!

Tarzan spread the word his way.
"Hey, everybody!" he shouted.
"We're having a contest!"

"Does he always have to yell?"
asked Tantor.

"The rules are easy,"
Terk told the animals.
"If you pick the most
bananas, you win."

The baboon went first.
He picked some bananas.
But he ate them, too!
"Peels don't count!" Terk shouted.

Tarzan got an idea.

The rhino tried.
He couldn't do it. He got stuck!
"Nice try, bud," Terk said.

The snake tried.
She couldn't do it.
She had no hands!

"NEXT!" Terk shouted.
More animals tried.
They couldn't do it either.

Tarzan worked on his idea
to get the most bananas.

"Go for it, Tantor,"
Terk said.
Tantor was about to
try when . . .
"EEEK! A LIZARD!"
Tantor was scared.
He bumped against
the tree and began to shake.
The tree shook, too.
And down came
ten bananas!

"My turn!" Terk said.
Terk climbed to the top.
She hung from a leaf
and began to pick.
". . . thirteen . . .
fourteen . . . fifteen . . ."
The stem snapped.
Terk and the bananas
fell down!

Tarzan had a plan.

"It's your turn, Tarzan," Terk said.
Tarzan didn't climb like a baboon,
slither like a snake,
or knock his head like a rhino.

Ready . . . aim . . . WHACK!

"Wow!" Terk said.

"You won."

"This contest was fun,"
Tarzan said.
"And we stayed out of trouble!"
Tantor said.

"Or maybe we didn't!"
Terk said.